How Do You Say I Love You, Dewey Dew?

Written by
Leslie Staub

Illustrated by
Jeff Mack

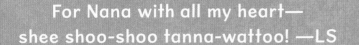

For Nana with all my heart—
shee shoo-shoo tanna-wattoo! —LS

For my Grandma Wood, with love. —JM

Text copyright © 2017 by Leslie Staub
Illustrations copyright © 2017 by Jeff Mack
All rights reserved.
For information about permission to reproduce selections
from this book, contact permissions@highlights.com.

Boyds Mills Press
An Imprint of Highlights
815 Church Street
Honesdale, Pennsylvania 18431
Printed in China
ISBN: 978-1-62979-497-6
Library of Congress Control Number: 2016960059

First edition
Design by Sara Gillingham Studio
The text of this book is set in Billy Serif, Brandon Printed,
Clarendon, School Script, and Sweater School.
The illustrations are done in pencil, watercolor, and digital media.
10 9 8 7 6 5 4 3 2 1

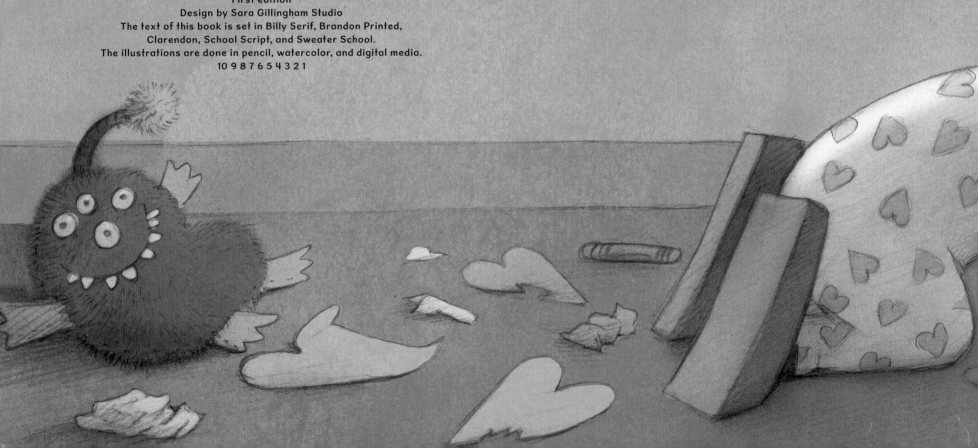

Click-Clack Waddle-Waddle
Dot-Dot Dewey Dew
from Planet Eight Hundred Seventy-
Two Point Nine was starting to love
life on Earth. Except he could not
pronounce the word—

LOVE

"Love," his mother said sweetly.

"**Wuhbuh!**" he repeated, trying his hardest.

"**Looove,**" she said slowly.
"**Wuh-*buh*,**" he said, "**wuhbuh, wuhbuh, wuhbuh!**"

"I hargle the English wanguage!"

"I know it's hard, Dewey," his mother said,
"but it's not right to hargle, not in any language."

Easy for *her* to say. *She* didn't have to go to school
with Brutus Auralias of the Second Grade.

"Hurgle glop,"

Dewey said as he climbed into bed.

"Don't worry, you'll get it!
Shee shoo-shoo tanna-wattoo,"
she said, and it sounded like
honey and birds' wings and
safety and singing.
He loved her too, but . . .

The next day, there was Brutus Auralias.
"Hey, Wubbah Boy, how do you say **'DUMBO'** in Alien?"

Dewey's urdle tightened. His eyeball squeezed.
Blue-black smoke rose dangerously from his hork.

Just as he was about to go ORBITAL, his
friends Melissa and J.J. came up beside him.
Dewey took a deep breath, counted to flork,
and decided not to BLOW.

"His language is called Eighty-N, not *ALIEN*," Melissa said.
"Yeah," J.J. added, "so shrishglit udious."
Which, by the way, means, *Be quiet you big bully* in Eighty-N.

Fortunately, Brutus Auralias
did not know that.

Back in *Ms. Brightsun's* first grade class, things were ootay until . . .
"Dewey, will you please read this word?" *Ms. Brightsun* asked.

"Wuhbuh," Dewey said under his breath.

LOVE

A few classmates started to laugh.
"Ooh, ooh, ooh!" Melissa said, raising her hand.
"The word is LOVE and Dewey is tired of being teased."

"Yeah," J.J. added.

Dewey blushed bright green.
His shoulders slumped.
His heart went glunk.
He wished he could disappear.

"AIR-WELL, EARTH-INGS! I AM OO-TAH-EAR!"

But that night he had
an even better idea!

Early the next morning, Dewey went straight to *Ms. Brightsun's* classroom so he could ask her a question without anyone else around.

"Happy Valentine's Day, class," *Ms. Brightsun* said. "Dewey has something wonderful to share with us."

With help from his friends, Dewey unrolled a big paper roll. On it, in amazing curlicue letters, were the words I LOVE YOU in Eighty-N with the English underneath.

"Dewey," *Ms. Brightsun* asked, "will you please tell the class how 'I love you' is said on Planet Eight Hundred Seventy-Two Point Nine?"

"shee shoo-shoo tanna-wattoo,"

he said, and it sounded like honey and birds' wings and courage and singing.

"Shee shoo-shoo tanna-wattoo!" he repeated.

It sounded like wanting and flowers and kindness and hoping. It sounded so funny-wonderful that the whole class wanted to try it.

It was hard at first.

"Shee shoo-shoo tooba-wooba."

"Shee too-too baba-wabba."

But soon the air was filled with a sound
like honey and birds' wings and sweetness and singing.

By the end of the day, everyone in the whole school was saying it.

Even Brutus Auralias. **"Me boo-boo wah-wah baba, ee oo-oo ba-ba ah-choo."** It didn't sound *quite* like honey or birds' wings or singing or anything.

But nobody minded.

Because, as their voices blended together, it was impossible not to wonder if maybe, just maybe, even Brutus Auralias of the Second Grade might someday live on a planet where the air is filled with a sound like honey and birds' wings and courage and caring and no one ever, ever, gets teased.

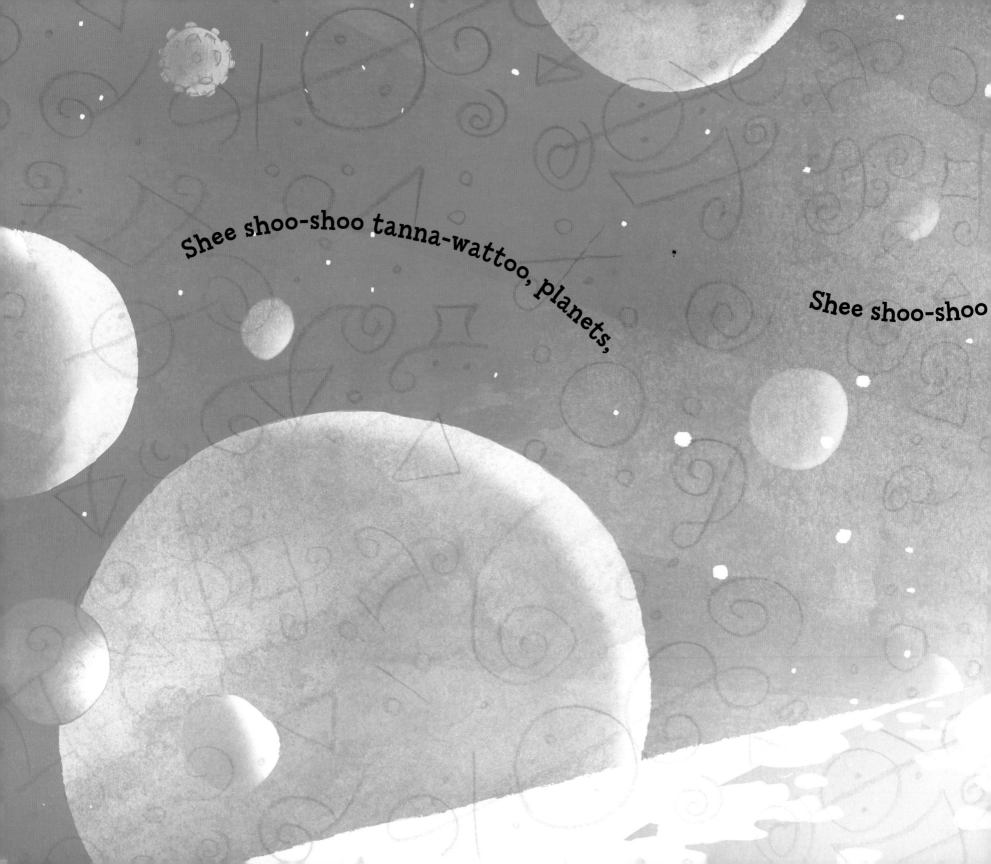

Shee shoo-shoo tanna-wattoo, planets,

Shee shoo-shoo

tanna-wattoo, stars,

Shee shoo-shoo tanna-wattoo, YOU—

—whoever, wherever, whatever you are!

5